The Queen's Bracelet

Collect all the Charmseekers –

The Queen's Bracelet
The Silver Pool

from April 2011
The Dragon's Revenge
A Tale of Two Sisters

from June 2011
The Fragile Force
The Stolen Goblet

from August 2011
The Magic Crystals
Secret Treasure

from October 2011
Star Island
Moonlight and Mermaids

from 2012
The Mirror of Deception
Zorgan and the Gorsemen
The Last Portal

www.charmseekers.co.uk

The Queen's Bracelet

Georgie Adams

Illustrated by Gwen Millward

Orion
Children's Books

First published in Great Britain in 2008
by Orion Children's Books
Reissued 2011 by Orion Children's Books
a division of the Orion Publishing Group Ltd
Orion House
5 Upper St Martin's Lane
London WC2H 9EA
An Hachette UK Company

1 3 5 7 9 8 6 4 2

A catalogue record for this book is available
from the British Library.

ISBN 978 1 4440 0289 8

Printed in Great Britain by CPI Mackays, Chatham, Kent

www.orionbooks.co.uk

For Norah Adams
– *A life lived to the full to the very end.*

N

SNOWFLAKE
MOUNTAINS

*Zorgan's
Tower*

HORSESHOE
BAY

THE ICE
COUNTRY

THE DA
FORES

THE
COINS

LANTERN
HILL

SHELL
BEACH

*Queen
Charm's
Palace*

*Morbrecia's
Castle*

TWO MOONS RIVER

THE GATEKEEPER

TROLL

STAR
ISLAND

The Thirteen Charms of Karisma

When Charm became queen of Karisma, the wise and beautiful Silversmith made her a precious gift. It was a bracelet. On it were fastened thirteen silver amulets, which the Silversmith called 'charms', in honour of the new queen.

It was part of Karisma law. Whenever there was a new ruler, the Silversmith made a special gift, to help them care for the world they had inherited. And this time it was a bracelet. She told Queen Charm it was magical because the charms held the power to control the forces of nature and keep everything in balance. She must take the greatest care of them. As long as she, and she alone, had possession of the charms, all would be well.

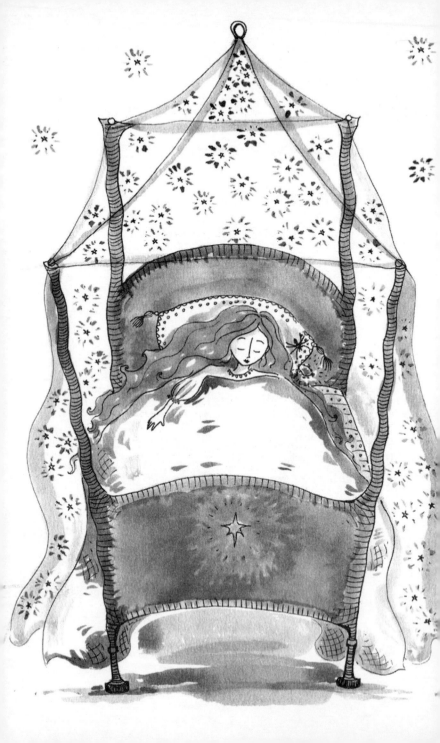

One

The two moons of Karisma shone brightly over the palace. Inside, Queen Charm slept peacefully, unaware of the enormous spider crawling over her bed.

The young queen had placed her charm bracelet under the pillow for safe-keeping. She had been warned to take care of it. And she did. So long as she had the bracelet, all would be well. The Silversmith had made that very clear. But should it fall into the wrong hands . . .

The spider moved swiftly. Silently it scuttled under the snow-white pillow, gripped its prize and eased the bracelet out. Thirteen silver charms glinted in the moonlight.

"Got it!" said the spider, Morbrecia. "Mine at last!"

The Silversmith wakes with a start.

"Something is wrong!" she tells herself.

She senses evil in the air. If the worst has happened . . . if, as she fears, the charm bracelet has fallen into the wrong hands . . . there will be consequences. Karisma will change. The laws of nature, so carefully held in balance by the magical bracelet, will fall apart.

"Hushish!* This is a bad business!"

Her sense of foreboding persists. It grips like a vice, tighter and tighter, until she is convinced the bracelet has been stolen. Who by? She has her suspicions. And, if she's right, it won't be easy getting it back!

She throws off the coverlet. Her gossamer robe shimmers like a shower of stars, as she crosses the room, to sit at her dressing table. A look of anxiety clouds her face. She brushes her hair vigorously, as if to rid herself of these terrible thoughts. She will go to the palace first thing in the morning to see Charm.

But first she must find someone to help look for what is lost. A seeker who will search far and wide. One who will care enough to carry out this quest and not give up, no matter what dangers lie ahead.

She rises and goes to the window, flings it wide

* *

✫ Hushish – a word used to express dismay

4

to breathe the chill night air. She gazes in wonder at the two moons casting their silvery-blue light – there's such a strange aura about them tonight! – and, away across the heavens, to the brightly shining Outworld* . . .

* *

✭ Outworld – the name Karismans call our world

5

"Quisto!"✳ she exclaims. "The box! How could I forget!"

How indeed! She recalls transporting herself to the Outworld to place a special box there. Few possess the magic power to 'transworld', as it is known, and even she had done so only once – to accomplish a secret mission. With her gift of foresight, she had predicted the box would serve a purpose in the Outworld, at some time in the future. Now it seems that the time has come.

The Silversmith closes her eyes, snaps her fingers, *click*! She's in a trance, 'seeing' far, far beyond the boundaries of Karisma. Who has the box? Who? Ah, yes! She breathes a sigh of relief. It's someone very special . . .

She has found her seeker!

* *
✳ Quisto – an exclamation of surprise

Two

Sesame Brown was munching a mouthful of muesli when she exploded.

"Dad! Did you know orangutans in Borneo are starving?"

A pumpkin seed flew across the breakfast table. It landed near her dad, Nic Brown, who was sitting opposite.

"Uh-huh," mumbled Nic, brushing the stray seed aside. He flicked through the pages of his newspaper. "It's here somewhere . . ."

Sesame looked up from reading *Wild About Wildlife* on the back of the cereal packet. She rolled her eyes.

"Dad, are you listening? This is serious!"

Nic put down his paper. Sesame was so like her mum, Poppy. She had Poppy's big brown eyes and Nic loved the way they flew wide open when she was cross. Like now.

Sesame went on reading.

"The rainforest which is their natural habitat is being cut down by unscru . . . un-*scrooo*-pu . . . "

"Unscrupulous?" offered Nic.

"Yes," said Sesame. "*Unscrupulous* timber operators, to clear the way for palm oil crops. The orangutans have no food and nowhere to live."

"How awful," said Nic, sneaking another look at his paper.

"AND," said Sesame, banging her spoon on the table to emphasise the point, "if something isn't done about it soon, wild orangutans will become EXTINCT!"

"Terrible!" agreed Nic.

The sudden *BANG* made him jump. He decided to give Sesame his full attention.

Again Nic was reminded of Poppy. She would have been as concerned about the orangutans as their daughter was now. And, when Sesame took an interest in something, she made it her business to find out all about it!

Poppy Brown had died in a car accident when Sesame was a baby. She had been a journalist, writing about the environment, climate change and things like that. And, like Sesame, she was crazy about animals — wild ones, tame ones, anything with whiskers, paws or claws. Not to mention ponies! Sesame was pony-mad too.

Just then Sesame's two little kittens, Chips and Pins, scampered across the floor.

"Oooo! Come here," she said, scooping them up and giving them a cuddle. The plight of the orangutan, it seemed, had been temporarily forgotten.

While Sesame stroked the kittens, Nic picked up his newspaper again. He found the photograph he was looking for.

"Look, Ses," he said. "Here's one of mine."

Nic was a photographer for THE DAILY TIMES. He was always rushing off to cover a news story. Sometimes, at weekends or in the holidays, he took Sesame with him.

Carefully, Sesame unhooked herself from the kittens' claws, and put them down to play. Then she looked at the picture. Three glamorous models wearing swirly skirts, tops and jackets were posing outside a new shop. **TIP TOPS** had just opened on the High Street.

"Oh Dad! Why didn't you take ME?" she wailed.

9

Sesame and her friend, Maddy, were seriously into fashion. "Tip Tops looks cooool!"

"Because I was there yesterday while you were at scho-o-o-o-o-l," he said.

"But today is Saturday!" said Sesame. "Can I go shopping with Maddy, Dad? PLEASE!"

"Ok," said Nic. "But don't stay out too long. I'm covering a football match this afternoon. But Lossy will be here, when you get back."

Lossy was Sesame's gran. Her real name was Lois, but when Sesame was little she'd called her Lossy and the name had stuck ever since. Sesame loved Lossy. Whenever her dad had to be away for work, Lossy was always there.

"Yippee!" sang Sesame, dancing round the kitchen. Chips and Pins thought this was a new game and pounced on her slippers.

"Ouch!" she squealed. "You've got sharp little claws!"

She ran upstairs to her room. It was right at the top of the house with low, sloping ceilings and a window. The walls were covered with Sesame's drawings (mostly ponies) and pictures of wild animals (mostly orangutans). And there was stuff all over the floor.

But Sesame liked it that way and knew where everything was. She skilfully hopped around a stack of CDs, two tops, a half-finished bead bangle, magazines and a pair of jelly pumps, to put on a CD. It was her favourite band, Crystal Chix. She sang

along while sweeping her long brown hair back with a hairband. Then she went to look in her wardrobe.

"What AM I going to wear?" She said with a sigh, staring at the jumble of clothes.

But it didn't take her long to choose a green stripy top to go with her jeans and funky trainers. After dressing in double-quick time, she grabbed her mobile and sat beside her bed. Her teddy Alfie flopped sideways on to the pillow. Propping him up

again, Sesame kissed his nose and switched on her
mobile. She sent a text to Maddy:

A few minutes later,
Maddy replied:

C U AT TIP
TO PS AT 10.
DNT B L8!
LOL SESAME
MWAH MWAH :)

GR8 C U
LUV MADDY
XX :)

"Great!" cried Sesame, jumping up and slinging a
large bag over her shoulder as she went out.

She was halfway through the door, when she
remembered her necklace. It was one she often wore
– a silver chain and locket, with tiny pictures of her
parents inside. It meant a lot to Sesame. She kept it
on her bedside table with some family photographs
and a jewellery box, which had
once belonged to her mum.

When Poppy died, Nic
had given the jewellery
box to Sesame. The lid
was beautifully painted,
with some strange
symbols round a circle.
Sesame was sure they
were some sort of code. Once

she'd asked her dad about it, but Nic had only shrugged and said, "No idea, Ses. I found that box in a junk shop. Just thought it looked special. I gave it to your mum when you were born. She loved it."

"So do I," Sesame told him. "But I wish I knew what those symbols meant."

"Well, knowing you," Nic had said, "you won't give up till you do!"

Sesame had pretended to peer at the lid through a magnifying glass, like a detective.

"Sesame Brown will track it down!" she'd said.

And they'd laughed.

Sesame picked up her necklace. It felt curiously warm, as if it had just been held. When she fastened the clasp, there was a tingle at the nape of her neck. She ran out of her room and down the stairs, two at a time. She found Nic checking his camera, ready for work.

"What time will you be home?" she asked.

"Sometime this evening," said Nic. "It's a late kick-off. I'll see you and Lossy later.

"Ok," she said, giving him a quick kiss. "Love you. Bye!"

Sesame walked along the pavement towards the High Street. Her best friend, Maddy Webb, lived on the other side of town and Sesame wished she lived closer. They did absolutely everything together.

At **TIP TOPS** Sesame checked her watch. Ten o'clock on the dot. She liked to be on time. She looked around for Maddy but she wasn't there. Surprise surprise, thought Sesame. Maddy was nearly always late!

There were lots of girls hurrying into the shop and Sesame longed to join them. Just then, she spotted Liz and Gemma. They saw her and came over.

"Hi, Sesame!" said Liz.

"Waiting for Maddy?" asked Gemma.

"Yeah," said Sesame. "We arranged to meet at ten. But you know Maddy!"

"Mmm!" said Liz, with a knowing grin.

"She's probably forgotten something and had to go back for it," said Gemma. "Maddy's SO forgetful!"

They all laughed, then Liz and Gemma went into **TIP TOPS** leaving Sesame to wait outside.

Sometimes Sesame got cross with Maddy for being late. Then they would fall out. But because they were best friends it never lasted for long. Maddy always said she was sorry, and they made up.

While she was waiting, Sesame looked in the window. There were some fabulous clothes! But one top seemed to stand out from all the rest. It was bright red with a sparkling heart.

She simply couldn't stop looking at it. And the more she looked, the more the heart seemed to . . . beat. Yes, beat! She was sure of it. How weird, thought Sesame.

The colours began to swirl. Round and round, faster and faster, until Sesame felt herself floating. And suddenly she floated right through the heart, into a silvery mist . . .

Three

The scream from Queen Charm's bedroom was shrill. It could be heard throughout the palace.

The piercing screech startled one sleepy guard wide-awake. Officer Dork raced to the royal apartment and found the queen in a state of shock. Her maid, Ozina, was trying to comfort her.

"What happened?" she asked.

"It was ghastly!" said Charm. "I thought I was dreaming. Something was crawling. Ugh! I saw, I'm sure I saw . . ."

She wasn't making much sense.

"Go on," said Ozina gently.

Dork stepped closer, to hear.

"A sp-sp-spider!" stuttered Charm. "An ENORMOUS spider. And it was stealing the bracelet!"

"Eeek!" squealed Ozina, jumping onto the bed. She was afraid the spider might still be on the floor. "I hate spiders!"

Dork rolled his eyes. Girls, eh! He thought the queen had probably imagined it all. She'd had a nightmare. Yes, that was it. But he managed to look

concerned as he asked:

"You say the intruder was a spider, Your Majesty?"

"Yes," said Charm. "A spider. But never mind that now. It's the BRACELET that matters!"

Both Dork and Ozina knew how important the bracelet was. Everyone in Karisma knew about the bracelet, with its thirteen lucky charms. So if it had been stolen . . .

Ozina peeped under the pillow. She knew Charm put the bracelet there every night. And, sure enough, it was missing.

With her mind now focused on the bracelet,

Charm regained her regal composure. Dork knew better than to underestimate this young and beautiful queen, for her fine, slender features concealed hidden strengths. Charm took her duties seriously and ruled her people well.

Dork stood smartly to attention, awaiting orders. He watched Charm cross the room to the window, to look out at the starry sky. Caught in the moonlight, her long, fair hair looked like a silvery waterfall, falling to her waist. How unlike her sister, Morbrecia, he thought. And an image of Morbrecia, with her wild, jet black hair and eyes, dark as the night, filled his head. He was in awe of Morbrecia. And just a little bit afraid . . .

His thoughts were interrupted by a courteous but firm command. Charm had turned to face him, clear what must be done.

"Officer Dork," she said. "Take a search party and find my bracelet. I must have it back!"

Four

Sesame landed with a *THUMP*! She found herself
sprawling on a patch of purple moss, staring at
two large, hairy feet.

"Who are YOU?" said a voice, from somewhere not
very far above her head.

Sesame looked up. A troll was standing near the
twisted trunk of a tree, looking very surprised.

"Er . . . Sesame Brown," said Sesame, in a daze. She
sat up, at eye-level with the troll, who was peering at
her intensely through bushy eyebrows.

"You're from the Outworld, aren't you?" he said.
Then he leaned a little closer to say, "I've heard all
about you Outworlders! But I never thought I'd meet
one. Why did you come?"

"What?" asked Sesame.

"The precise nature of your visit?" said the troll, a
little irritably. "In other words, what . . . are . . . you

19

doing . . . here?" He said it slowly, as if Sesame was stupid.

"I haven't a clue," she said. Which was true. "Anyway, who are you? Where am I?"

"Tssh!" muttered the troll. "You don't know much, do you? I'm Gatekeeper One. And you've just barged into Karisma."

"Gatekeeper? Kar-is-ma? Where's that?"

Sesame was utterly bewildered, though she was beginning to remember being whisked off her feet and spun round, like clothes in a washing machine. There were so many questions she wanted to ask but she found herself saying:

"How many gates are there?"

"Twelve, of course," said the troll. "Twelve gates. Twelve gatekeepers." Then he added with a grin: "Lucky you came through mine. I'm one of the nice ones. Get it? ONE of the nice ones!"

"Y-e-e-e-s," said Sesame. It was obviously one of his favourite jokes. "And the others?" she asked, curious to know about those, too.

"You don't want to tangle with some of them!" said the troll, wiping a hairy hand across his brow. "Let me see. There's a one-eyed giant at number Four. Foul temper he's got. And the monster at number Eleven likes to eat his visitors. He calls them . . . his elevenses!"

And suddenly he burst out laughing.

Tears rolled down his cheeks and his belly shook. Sesame giggled nervously.

Eventually, the gatekeeper stopped laughing and gave her a map. He stamped it with the words:

Outworlder - Tourist

He handed it to her saying:

"Map of Karisma. Gate closes at sunset. Don't be late and watch out for gribblers!"

"What are gribblers?" asked Sesame, taking a quick look over her shoulder. There was no reply. The gate-keeper had disappeared. He'd simply vanished.

"Huh! He wasn't very helpful!" said Sesame, nervously fiddling with her necklace. The locket suddenly sprang open and there were the tiny pictures of her parents, smiling back at her. Seeing her dad and her mum made her feel much better.

"Right," she said decisively, snapping the locket shut and opening the map. "Karisma, here I come! But I hope I don't meet any gribblers, whatever they are!"

As she wandered slowly along a narrow path, Sesame looked at the map. She reckoned she was in the Dark Forest, which was clearly marked. She could also make out a speck of light on the map. It appeared to be moving in the direction she was going. To try it out, she zigzagged across the path and, sure enough, the light tracked her movements exactly.

"Cool!" said Sesame. "A magic map!"

Now she looked around, fascinated by everything she saw. Creepers grew before her eyes, coiling long tentacles round trees, like snakes; jagged shoots shot up through the undergrowth; bare bushes suddenly burst into leaf. The forest was alive! It seemed everything was waking up to the early morning sunlight, filtering through the branches.

And the air was full of sounds. As Sesame went deeper into the forest, she heard the hollow knocking of a beak on wood; the noisy chatter of unseen birds; the *whoop-whoop!* call of a strange animal; the crackle of shrivelled leaves underfoot . . .

Sesame had just stopped to take a look at a gigantic tree with blue spotted leaves, when *Whoop-whoop! Whoop-whoop!* Something with spiky pink fur crashed down from above.

Terrified, Sesame jumped back.

"Are you a gri-gri–gribbler?" she asked.

But the creature, which had landed at her feet, just stared at her with its big round eyes. They looked sad. *Whoop-whoooo!* it cried, in a pitiful way. And Sesame immediately felt sorry for it.

"Oh, you poor thing!" she said. "I don't care even if you ARE a gribbler. You look like a baby who's lost its mother. I'll help you, if I can. My name's Sesame," she said. "What's yours?"

"Fig," said Fig, who had just learnt to say his name and liked the sound of it.

"Well, come on, Fig, let's go and find your mother!" she said.

And Fig *whooped* and looked much happier.

The two set off together through the forest, with Fig holding tight to Sesame's hand. Fig seemed to trust her completely, which made Sesame feel very responsible. Besides, she loved a challenge! Sesame Brown was never happier than when she was solving a problem.

Glancing at the map to see where they were, she now saw *two* specks of light – one slightly bigger than the other.

"Look," she said to Fig, "that's us. And there's a palace!"

Sesame clambered on to a rock, to get a better view. There! She could just make out the palace in the distance, with the sun glinting on its towers. She had a good look round for Fig's mother too. Disappointingly, there wasn't another pink creature in sight. But she was curious to see a group of soldiers in smart red and gold uniforms, nearby. They appeared to be searching for something too. Some were crawling over tangled roots, while others peered into bushes.

Sesame jumped off the rock. One of the soldiers spotted her and stepped forward. It was Dork. He eyed Sesame suspiciously. She's not from these parts! he thought.

"Name?" Dork barked the question.

And when Sesame told him, Dork asked her sarcastically:

"Looking for something, Sesame Brown?"

"Yes!" said Sesame, eagerly. She thought the soldier might help. "Fig has lost its mother. Have you seen any of . . . these? Do you know what they're called?"

Dork knew very well.

"Tunganoras," he said, dismissively. "We get a lot of them round here. But I've got more important things to do. I suppose you and your furry friend haven't, by any chance, come across a bracelet?"

"No," said Sesame. "Have you lost one?"

"*I* haven't," said Dork, "but Queen Charm has.

Her Majesty's charm bracelet was stolen last night."

"Oh dear!" said Sesame. But an exciting idea had just whizzed into her head. Supposing *I* could be the one to find the queen's bracelet? Wow! Maybe that's why I'm here? "Leave it to me," she said, helpfully. "Sesame Brown will track it down!" And she meant every word.

But Dork thought she was joking and was in no mood for funny remarks.

"Queen Charm's bracelet is a bit special," he said briskly. "It must be found and returned as soon as possible!"

"Right!" said Sesame. "I'll do my best. Any idea who stole it?"

Dork looked uneasy.

"It was stolen by a spider," he said quietly. "A whopping great SPIDER!"

Five

The soaring column of black rock, which was Zorgan's Tower, rose from the barren landscape, like a cobra ready to strike. From his Star Room, high at the top, the magician used a powerful telescope to study the heavens above – and spy on people below.

It was here the sorcerer waited impatiently for Morbrecia to return. He paced round and round, fiddling with a gold medallion. Rings glittered on every finger. Zorgan loved bright things. And soon he would have Charm's exquisite bracelet to add to his collection. He was beside himself with anticipation!

To pass the time, he amused himself remembering how this had all come about. It had been so easy persuading Morbrecia to fall in with his plans. And, as for turning her into a spider . . . Morbrecia had loved that!

27

A spider stealing from her sister who was terrified of creepy-crawlies. Vixee!✶

✶ **Vixee** – a gleeful, triumphant exclamation meaning great or wicked

Suddenly, Zorgan's thoughts were interrupted. Something was being dragged slowly across the floor. He listened and looked down. There she was!

Zorgan smirked. Morbrecia trusted him completely. "I'll make you greater than Queen Charm," he had promised. "Bring me the bracelet and I'll empower it with dark magic – SO much more dangerous and exciting! You'll have such fun creating havoc and mayhem!"

A likely story! Zorgan intended to keep it for himself. The Silversmith had cast each lovely charm. They had special powers. Besides, the bracelet was fabulous! It was only right HE should be the one to wear it. Zorgan stretched out his hand . . .

"Not so fast!" said Morbrecia, dangling the bracelet from a spidery leg. She wasn't silly. "Undo the spell. Then you can have it."

The sorcerer was taken by surprise. He hadn't bargained for this. His plan had been to grab the charm bracelet and squash Morbrecia flat! Finish her off. Squish, squish. Bye-bye. She was nothing but trouble anyway.

Now he was afraid she might just scuttle off. Hide the precious bracelet somewhere out of reach. It was a tricky situation. He must take care! Zorgan squeezed a smile from his lips. Then he said sweetly:

"Trust me, Morbrecia. You know I only want to

help. I'll make you powerful. You'll be queen instead of Charm. Think of it! *Queen* Morbrecia!"

Morbrecia had to admit, it did sound good.

"Fairsay,"* she replied. "But fix this spell or else . . ."

Zorgan couldn't risk arguing. Quickly he chanted:

"ADIN CHARA, CHARAN IDAR.
ARACH NIDA — VASHOOM!"

* *

⭐ Fairsay – ok, all right

There was a blinding green flash as the spell broke, and Morbrecia was herself once more.

For a tantalizing few minutes, Morbrecia toyed with the bracelet. She turned it round and round, delighted by each charm: a lucky horseshoe, for a unicorn perhaps?; a coin for good fortune; a lantern to light the way; the daintiest snowflake . . . She couldn't wait to wear it! But she was greedy and ambitious too. If there was a chance Zorgan could work his magic . . . If he could *really* make the bracelet super-powerful . . .

"Enough!" cried Zorgan, suddenly snatching the bracelet. "Foolish girl! If you thought for a moment I'd let you have it, you are very much mistaken."

And he put it on. One of the charms was a heart with a little lock. Another was a tiny key. Together they fastened the bracelet securely round his wrist. Zorgan stretched out his wrist and, for a fleeting moment, there was a look of ecstasy on his face. Each silver charm glistened so brightly! Strange. He had expected the bracelet to feel cool. But no! It was warm, and getting warmer. Then it turned HOT! Scorching, burning, blazing hot. The charms shimmered with heat.

"OwwwWWOOOOOOO!" howled Zorgan.

Morbrecia stood transfixed by this turn of events. She was fascinated! Perhaps, she thought, the bracelet recognised her as its rightful owner? Was it teaching Zorgan a lesson for tricking her? Yes! That was it! She stood and watched as Zorgan leaped around in agony, tearing at the burning band.

"Horrid, horrid thing! Get off!" he screamed, desperate to be rid of it. He clawed at the clasp, yelling as it burnt his fingers, until *SNAP!* The clasp broke and Zorgan wrenched the bracelet off.

Morbrecia was convinced the bracelet wouldn't burn her. It was rightfully hers! Surely it would cool as soon as SHE touched it? Seizing her chance, she lunged forward. But she was too late.

As Zorgan wrenched the bracelet apart, he flung it with *such* force that twelve of the thirteen charms broke off. They flew far and wide, all over Karisma. But the heart clung to the bracelet. They remained together.

Six

"*Whoop-whoop!*" cried Fig.

It was some time since Sesame and the tunganora had left Dork and his men, searching for the bracelet. Sesame had been walking along, deep in thought. First there were the gribblers the gatekeeper had warned her about. What *were* they? Where did they hang out? Then, and much more intriguing, was this news about a spider stealing a bracelet! And who was Queen Charm? Sesame was now convinced that she had been sent to Karisma to find the missing bracelet . . .

Whoop-whoop!

The cry suddenly jolted Sesame back to the present. She'd almost forgotten about Fig!

The tunganora was tugging at her arm and pointing to some blue leaves, growing at the top of a tall tree.

"Hungry?" said Sesame, stopping to comfort him.

Fig responded by sucking his paws noisily.

"R-i-g-h-t," she said, looking up between the branches. "So, you want *those* leaves and you'd like me to get them?"

Whoop! They understood each other perfectly! It was a bit scary but eventually Sesame managed to climb to the top and bring down a handful of leaves. After hastily eating them all, Fig gave a joyful *whoop!* and turned a somersault. Sesame laughed.

"Come on," she said cheerfully, "your mum can't be far away." She hoped she was right.

Shortly afterwards, they came to a clearing where a lot of trees had been cut down. There were fallen tree trunks and twisted branches everywhere! Sesame didn't think the map would be much use here, so she put it away in her pocket. She led Fig through the tangled undergrowth, stepping over logs and ducking under boughs. They were making slow but steady progress, until they tripped on some sticks . . . *SNAP! CRACK!*

"Whoooaaaaar!" yelled Sesame.

"*Whooooo!*" cried Fig.

They had fallen into a pit. Luckily their fall was broken by something soft and hairy. Something PINK and hairy.

"Moomoo!"* cried Fig, joyfully. He had found his mother.

Recovering from her fall, Sesame stood up and introduced herself to Fig's mother. At first the tunganora was nervous, but eventually Sesame discovered that her name was Hob.

And now that Fig and Hob had been happily reunited, she set about getting everyone out of the pit.

Although the pit wasn't very deep, Sesame could see there was no way a tunganora could escape from

it on its own. This was obviously a trap! Sesame was worried that whoever made it might return at any minute and find them.

Sesame crouched down.

"Quick!" she said to Hob, "stand on me. I'll pass Fig up when you're out."

* * * * * * * * * * *

★ Moomoo – mother

35

Fortunately it didn't take long for Hob to realise that Sesame was trying to help. So she jumped on Sesame's shoulders and climbed out easily. Then, when Fig had been rescued, Hob reached down and hoisted Sesame to the top.

"Who do you think did this?" asked Sesame, clambering over the edge.

"Gribblers!" replied Hob, speaking at last. She spat the word out in disgust.

"Mmm!" said Sesame. "I've heard about them. Who are they?"

"Vile creatures!" said Hob. "Sharp teeth. Bad breath!"

"And the trap?" queried Sesame.

"To catch us . . ." Hob said.

But she was careful not to frighten Fig by saying what would have happened, if they had.

"They want our trees," she explained. "It's the leaves, you see? They'll do anything for the leaves." Hob picked up a few wilted ones that had been left lying on the ground.

"To eat?" asked Sesame.

"No!" said Hob. "They make potions. They think it makes them strong."

At the sight and mention of his favourite food, Fig started up an insistent *Whoop-whoop-whooping* wail. He was obviously still hungry. So, after thanking Sesame for her help, Hob and Fig went off in search of fresh leaves.

As Sesame watched them go, she thought the plight of the tunganora sounded familiar. Their trees were being cut down by greedy gribblers. Their food and habitat was being destroyed. Something she'd heard or read maybe? But she couldn't quite remember now.

Sesame looked at her watch. The troll had warned her to be back at the gate by sunset, and she didn't want to be late. But wow! Something strange had happened. The dial on her watch had changed. Instead of numbers, there were pictures of the sun, moon and stars.

"What's going on?" said Sesame.

At first she hadn't a clue how to tell the time with it. Then she noticed the sun was slowly going down.

"Oh, I get it," she said. "When the sun goes behind the hill . . . it's sunset. Funky!"

She reckoned she had about an hour left to explore, before it was time to go.

Seven

"AAAARH!" screamed Morbrecia, as the bracelet and charms scattered in all directions. Her dark eyes flashed with fury.

"That was mine!" she yelled at Zorgan. "Mine, you MAGWORT!"✻

Zorgan winced. He rubbed the place on his wrist where the charms had burned. Besides, he hated being called a magwort. That really hurt.

"Out!" he cried. "Get out!"

"I'm going!" said Morbrecia. "But I'll get those charms back! Then you'll be sorry. I'll find them and DESTROY you!"

"On the contrary," said Zorgan. His tone was quiet but chilling. "You're the one who'll be sorry, Morbrecia. I'll make very sure of THAT!"

Morbrecia raced from Zorgan's tower. As she ran through shrouds of early morning mist, her black robes flapped like bats' wings. She was heading for the Dark Forest, to meet up with the gribblers. She'd get them to help her.

* *

✻ Magwort — probably the worst name you could call anyone! General term for a fool

39

Even as she took a shortcut past Queen Charm's palace, she was still spitting with rage at Zorgan's trickery. And the sight of her sister's palace did nothing to improve her temper.

"I went to all that trouble to steal the bracelet," Morbrecia hissed through clenched teeth, "and that slitey★ sorcerer throws it away!"

Entering the forest, Morbrecia came to a curtain of creepers. The writhing tentacles caught in her hair and she had to wrestle her way through.

★ Slitey – sly or untrustworthy

40

"Balam* weeds!" she cursed them. "Out of my way!"

It was eerily still among the trees, broken only by the sudden *swish!* of dry leaves, as an animal scuttled to hide. It was as if the forest was holding its breath in fear.

Morbrecia was hurrying along a twisty path, when Officer Dork and his search party appeared. They were returning to the palace after an unsuccessful morning. Dork was dreading telling Queen Charm they hadn't found the bracelet. But when he saw Morbrecia, he brightened up. Meeting her, by chance, had made his day.

"Princess Morbrecia," he said bowing low. "How mice to feet you!"

The words came out all wrong and he blushed bright red. To make matters worse, his men had begun to snigger.

"What?" snapped Morbrecia. She'd never liked Dork. She thought he was a creep.

He began again.

"I s-s-said how m-m-mice to . . ."

An awkward silence followed before Dork tried once more. He'd thought of a piece of news that might interest her.

* *

★ Balam – cursed, an angry exclamation

"We've been searching for the queen's bracelet," he said. "It was stolen last night."

"Really," said Morbrecia flatly.

It wasn't *quite* the response he'd expected. So he leaned closer and added, "By a SPIDER!" Dork had high hopes this last detail might result in Morbrecia squealing with fright. But it didn't work out that way. Morbrecia's eyes positively glowed with excitement.

"Did it scare her?" she asked.

"Queen Charm was frightened out of her royal wits," replied Dork.

"Vixee!" exclaimed Morbrecia, gleefully.

And an idea suddenly struck her. Dork might be a creep but he could be a useful one. She smiled at him.

"If you find the bracelet or . . ." she hesitated. She must be careful not to say too much. If she revealed that the charms had been scattered – he'd be suspicious.

He'd want to know how she knew. So she finished in a vague sort of way. ". . . you know, find anything. You'll tell me won't you? We must all do our best to find the bracelet and return it to . . . its rightful owner, mustn't we?"

How cleverly Morbrecia concealed her true intentions! And Dork didn't suspect a thing. He bowed again and said:

"Of course! Anything for you, Princess Morbrecia."

It suddenly occurred to him to mention his meeting with Sesame Brown, earlier that morning. He slightly altered the facts, to make it sound as if he'd ordered the Outworlder to search for the bracelet. Dork thought Morbrecia would be impressed. Instead she was furious.

"Blatz!" ★ she exclaimed. "You can't trust an Outworlder! What if this Sesame Brown finds the bracelet? Supposing she keeps it? What then? Keep looking, Dork!" she ordered. "We've got to find the bracelet before SHE does!"

And with that, Morbrecia stormed off to meet the gribblers.

* * * * * * * * * * * * * * * * * * * *
★ Blatz – a really angry exclamation

Eight

A hedge towered above her. Sesame had left the
Dark Forest and arrived in front of an enormous
wall of green. From somewhere high above came the
sound of hedge clippers.

Snip-snip. Snip-snip. Snip-snip!

Sesame craned her neck to look up. At the top, she
saw two gardeners clipping the topiary. From where
Sesame was standing they looked tiny. One gardener
was clipping a cat, with a long curled tail. The other
was shaping a dolphin.

When they caught sight of Sesame, they looked
very surprised. But they seemed friendly.

"Helloo!" called one.

"Fairday!"* said the other, waving his shears.

"Hi!" said Sesame. She was curious about the topiaries. "What are they?" she asked.

"Each represents a charm on the queen's bracelet," said the first gardener, who was now skilfully trimming the cat's tail.

"I see," said Sesame. "How many are there?"

"Thirteen!" shouted the second, giving the dolphin one last *snip!*

Sesame looked along the top of the hedge. From where she was standing she could see a crescent moon, star, seashell, horseshoe and a butterfly. There were others but they were too far away to see clearly.

"Can I see them all?" asked Sesame, eager to find out more about the bracelet.

And the gardeners, who were only too pleased to show off their work, allowed Sesame into the palace gardens. She found a gap in the hedge, by a ladder, just wide enough for her to squeeze through.

* * * * * * * * * * * * * * *
✯ Fairday– a typical
Karisman friendly greeting

On the other side the gardens seemed to go on for ever. The palace looked very grand, with a lake and fountain playing, nearby. There were colourful flowers everywhere, and some statues too.

"Wow!" exclaimed Sesame.

It all looked so amazing. She set off along a path, past some strange-looking plants. Over there was a pumpkin patch with the funkiest fruits Sesame had ever seen. A purple pumpkin was popping seeds.

"Cool!" she cried, nimbly catching a pumpkin seed in mid-flight. It tasted good, so she caught and nibbled some more as she wandered along. In a while, the path divided.

"Which way now? Left or right?" she said aloud.

She decided right and, almost immediately, came to the entrance of a maze. It was as if something had guided her there, and was telling her to go inside! But she thought to check her watch before she went in.

By this time the sun had reached the top of the hill. Sesame calculated, as best she could, there was about half an hour to sunset. I'll be quick, she thought. I'm good at mazes. And who knows what I might find!

The paths went round in circles. First Sesame walked down a long path and turned left. Then left again. Now right. On and on and round and round – this way and that – until at last . . .

"Yesssss!" Sesame congratulated herself proudly. She had found the heart of the maze. It was the smallest circle of all and in the middle was a large pot, planted with flowers. Sesame thought they looked like poppies. And for a reason she couldn't think of, they reminded her of someone . . .

Sesame stopped daydreaming and snatched another look at her watch. True, she'd found the middle pretty quickly, but she still had to find her way out. Now she'd have to hurry. She was about to leave when something shiny caught her eye. A silvery object was caught up in the poppies. Carefully, she pulled the flowers apart and reached in . . .

It was the missing bracelet!

"Oh!" she gasped. It was beautiful. But there was only one charm on it – a tiny heart with a lock. She turned the bracelet around and counted twelve more rings where the other charms should have been. What a shame! thought Sesame. Perhaps they've fallen in here?

She peered into the poppies again. No, nothing there.

"Right," she said. "One bracelet. One charm. It's a start. Now for the other twelve!"

Sesame was determined to find all the charms for the queen. In fact, she would make it her mission to succeed! She'd be a . . . *Charmseeker*. Yes! That was it. She said it aloud:

"Charmseeker!"

And it sounded just right.

Sesame put the bracelet in her pocket – the one where she'd put her map – but now she discovered it wasn't there. "Oh no!" she cried. "I must have dropped it somewhere." But there was no time to worry about that now. She must find her way out of the maze and get to the gate before it closed.

Can you find the path Sesame took to get to the centre of the maze and out again?

nine

An order had been issued from the palace to the twelve gatekeepers of Karisma. It read:

> **Stolen!**
> The bracelet belonging to Her Majesty Queen Charm was stolen last night from the palace. The identity of the intruder is unknown, but it is believed to be a large spider. Gatekeepers are ordered to report any spider seen acting suspiciously.
> It is of the utmost importance that the bracelet and its thirteen charms are returned to Her Majesty.
> By Order. *Palace Secretary*

At dawn the Silversmith had been to the palace, to warn the queen of her fears.

"Zorgan's behind this," she began angrily. "I just know it!" She tossed her long, silvery hair to one side. "There's so much at stake. If he has the bracelet, well . . . I dread to think of the consequences!"

50

Charm was only too well aware. She felt angry and upset that this could have happened, here at the palace, surrounded by all her guards!

"I did my best to protect it!" she said.

"I know," said the Silversmith, gently. "You're not to blame. No one could have done more to keep it safe. But even you are powerless against the forces of evil that were here last night!"

The Silversmith frowned. How could she tell Charm that she had a nagging feeling her sister was involved somehow? The ugly thought had been buzzing round her head like a fly, ever since she had awoken last night, convinced that the bracelet had been stolen. And it had. But she had no proof about Morbrecia. Was that just intuition?

She decided, for the time being, to keep these thoughts to herself and quickly changed the subject. She had some good news.

"I've found someone who can help," she said.

"Who?" asked Charm.

"Sesame Brown," said the Silversmith. "A Charmseeker. She arrived this morning."

The queen was intrigued. She'd never heard of a Charmseeker before, let alone met one.

"I should like to meet Sesame Brown," she said. "Please, invite her to the palace."

"I can't do that," said the Silversmith. She must choose her words carefully. Losing the charm bracelet was bad enough. But she also knew the charms had been scattered. For, at the very moment Zorgan had so ruthlessly cast the charms away, the Silversmith had felt a wrenching pain. "I'm afraid you can't see her until the bracelet . . . the charms . . . everything's been found."

"Why?" said Charm, sounding disappointed. Then she added, wryly. "After all, I am the Queen! Surely you can grant me that wish?"

"Your Majesty," replied the Silversmith firmly, "Sesame must be left to work in her own way. In her own time. She has a special gift, you see? The gift to *seek*."

The queen didn't really understand but she knew it was no good arguing with the Silversmith. She had her own way of doing things. Besides, she trusted her completely.

"Then I'll just have to be patient, won't I," she said with a sigh. "But it all sounds very mysterious!"

When the Silversmith returned home, she lit thirteen candles and named them after the charms.

They were magic candles – each one would burn until its charm had been found – however long it took.

The gribblers were furious! Three of them were standing around the empty pit, dribbling and cursing. The biggest of them, Varg, bared his teeth. They were a disgusting shade of yellow and some were missing altogether.

"Shumone's been meshing wiv our shtuff," he said, showering the others with a spray of slime. "You can shmell 'em!"

"Yeah!" said another, called Gorz. He sniffed noisily.

"Poooeee!" exclaimed the youngest one, Bod.

It was remarkable the gribblers could smell anything apart from their own awful stench. Their breath smelled like rotting fish – only ten times worse. Varg spoke again.

"I knows we had one," he growled. Heard it go down. Should've shorted it meshelf. Bet it were a biggun!"

Varg was, of course, talking about Hob. It made him mad as a maggot to think that someone had released a tunganora from the trap. Just when they were doing their best to get rid of them! Those wretched pink creatures lived off the leaves they wanted, to make potions.

He spat out a dollop of slime that whizzed down into the pit. It landed on something at the bottom with a resounding *SPLAT!*

"What's that?" said Gorz, peering over the side. He had sharp, piggy eyes. "There's something down there. Look!"

Bod jumped into the pit, then scrambled out again, clutching something in his hand. It was Sesame's map!

"Give it here!" said Varg, snatching the map and cuffing Bod round the ear, because he felt like it.

At that precise moment Morbrecia arrived. The

gribblers shuffled awkwardly as she approached.

"What's that?" she demanded.

Varg handed her the map. Morbrecia scowled when she read what the gatekeeper had written:

Outworlder - Tourist

"So!" she snarled. "Sesame Brown has been here! She's a meddler, make no mistake!"

She still couldn't believe how stupid Dork had been, for telling this stranger about the bracelet!

As soon as Gorz heard the word Outworlder, he held his nose.

"I knew it!" he cried. "Dats wot de smell woz. It's right up by dose!" Then he sneezed.

A-H-H-H-TISHOOOO!

It was not a pretty sight.

Varg scowled.

"Shees been meshing in our bishness!" he explained to Morbrecia, who had ducked to avoid the spit. "I'll shkewer her shkull!" he hissed.

"I'll boil her brains!" said Gorz.

"I'll have her eyeballs for lollipops!" said Bod.

A cold smile escaped from Morbrecia's lips. She could always rely on the gribblers to cheer her up.

"Good!" she said. "Sniff her out. Let's be rid of her! And there's something else. I need your help to find a bracelet . . ."

Ten

Sesame came out of the maze and ran to the hedge. She was starting to panic. The sun was going down fast and soon it would be sunset. What if she got to the gate too late? What if it was closed? What if . . . ?

"Oh stop what iffing!" she told herself crossly. "THINK!"

Where was the gap? She quickly looked along the bottom of the hedge, from side to side. But it was like a solid wall – not a gap or gate to be seen!

She tried to remember the spot where she'd seen the two gardeners working on some topiary.

The gap was near there. One had been clipping a . . . what was it? Then she remembered. A cat! "Easy peasey," she said. "Find the cat and I'm out."

Sesame expected to spot it straightaway but she didn't. Instead she found herself near where she'd first spotted the other topiaries – but then they'd been too far away to see clearly. Close up, she could now see these were a heart, a key, a cloverleaf, a snowflake and a lantern. And what was that round one? A coin? Sesame remembered that each neatly clipped shape represented one of the thirteen charms.

But where was the cat?

Sesame looked carefully around the enormous hedge. And there, quite a long way off, she could just make out a dolphin and . . . the CAT! She ran as fast as she could until she found the gap. Then she scrambled through, back into the Dark Forest.

It looked different somehow. The setting sun cast a pinkish glow over everything. Sesame wished she still had the map! She had just started to walk, when Hob appeared. She'd been waiting to show Sesame the way.

"One good turn deserves another," she told Sesame. "Quick! Come with me. The gribblers are out to get you!"

This alarming piece of news took Sesame completely by surprise.

"How do they know about me?" she asked.

As they hurried through the forest Hob explained how this unfortunate situation had come about. She told Sesame she had overheard three gribblers talking.

"They found your map," said Hob. "You dropped it down the pit."

"Ah!" said Sesame. "So that's where it went."

"Morbrecia's got it now," said Hob. She was lolloping along at a steady pace and Sesame was doing her best to keep up. She could feel the bracelet jiggling about in her pocket and she didn't want to lose it.

"Who's Morbrecia?" she asked, a bit out of breath.

"Queen Charm's sister," said Hob. "Princess Morbrecia. Mixes with the likes of Zorgan and the gribblers. Bit of a witch, if you ask me."

Sesame was confused. Who was Zorgan? And why was Morbrecia like a witch? She was about to ask, when Hob stopped dead in her tracks. She sniffed.

"Fish," she whispered.

"In a forest!" said Sesame.

Then she got wind of it too. A disgusting smell of rotting fish filled the air.

"Ugh!" she said, holding her nose.

"Sssh!" said Hob. "Gribbler!"

In the dim light of the forest, against an ever reddening sky, Sesame saw a hideous creature. It

58

was Varg and he was heading slowly their way. Sesame wanted to scream. She cupped her hands over her mouth, her stomach churning like a blender.

Varg's hooded eyes had picked out two shadowy shapes among the trees. Hob could have told Sesame a useful thing or two about gribblers. She knew that their sense of smell and hearing remained good at all times. But at dusk their eyesight is poor. Their hooded eyes can't adjust to the change of light. But this was no time for a lecture on gribblers. Instead she whispered urgently:

"Look! There's the gate."

Sesame looked. She reckoned the gate was about twenty paces away. And she saw the troll preparing to lock it. It was nearly sunset! Hob kept her eyes on Varg.

"I'll deal with *him*," she said "Now run for it. Fast as you can. GO!"

And Sesame ran.

Had she looked back she would have seen Hob crashing through the undergrowth, dangerously near the gribbler.

Sesame raced on, her heart pounding. The troll had put the key in the lock and was about to turn it.

"Wait!" cried Sesame. "Oh, please WAIT!"

"You're late!" said the troll. He stood, arms folded, foot tapping. He pointed to a notice from the palace and Sesame read it:

Stolen!
The bracelet belonging to Her Majesty Queen Charm was stolen last night from the palace. The identity of the intruder is unknown, but it is believed to be a large spider. Gatekeepers are ordered to report any spider seen acting suspiciously.
It is of the utmost importance that the bracelet and its thirteen charms are returned to Her Majesty.
By Order. Palace Secretary

Sesame was very afraid the troll wouldn't let her through if he knew she had the bracelet – and there wasn't time to explain about her mission now!

So she said nothing and he opened the gate.

"Next time, don't be LATE!" he said.

And 'late' was the very last word Sesame heard, as she fell, fell, fell into a silvery mist . . .

Eleven

"LATE! . . . late!"

"What?" said Sesame, her head in a spin.

"I said, I'm sorry I'm *late*!" Maddy was saying. "I tried to get here on time. Honestly, Sessy. But I forgot my purse and had to . . ."

"Yeah. Fine, fine," said Sesame.

She was bemused to find herself back outside **TIP TOPS** on the High Street. She glanced at her watch. The sun, moon and stars had gone. Her watch was back to normal. It was just five past ten. Maddy thought Sesame was checking to see how late she was.

"I know you're cross," she said. "But I did try!"

"No. I'm not," said Sesame.

And she flung her arms round Maddy and hugged her.

"Oh, Maddy, I'm SO pleased you're here," she said. "I've got so much to tell you!"

"R-i-g-h-t . . ." said Maddy, wondering what was coming next. Sesame looked as if she was going to burst. "You haven't got a crush on a *boy* or something?"

"No way!" said Sesame, pulling a face. "Something . . . more exciting. But it'll have to wait."

"Oh, that's not fair!" complained Maddy. "We never have secrets. We tell each other everything!"

Sesame knew she *would* tell Maddy sometime. But not now. She'd find the right moment to tell her friend about an extraordinary place called Karisma. That's if it DID exist!

"I will, I *promise*," said Sesame. "Look," she said, quickly changing the subject and pointing to the window. "I've just seen this fabulous top . . . "

Sesame stopped. She couldn't believe her eyes. The top with the silvery heart wasn't there.

"Which one?" asked Maddy.

"Er . . . it's gone," said Sesame, flatly.

Her head still felt a bit funny. Had she imagined everything? She was so sure it had all started here. Maddy rolled her eyes.

"You're acting weird today!" she said, slipping her arm through Sesame's. "Come on. Let's go in."

When Sesame got home that afternoon, she raced upstairs to her room. She took the bracelet, with its one remaining charm, out of her pocket, to look at it.

"Oh dear!" she sighed, cradling the tiny heart in her hand. She was more determined than ever to go back to Karisma, to look for the other charms. "I haven't a clue how to get back there," she confided in her teddy, Alfie. "But I'm a Charmseeker, see? I'll find a way!"

Until then, Sesame would have to keep the bracelet safe and she knew just the place. The jewellery box, beside her bed! She knew it had a tray, which was divided into thirteen little sections, with a larger one in the middle.

"Perfect!" she said, carefully placing the bracelet and the heart inside the box. She felt strangely excited, seeing them there. Her mission had just begun!

"One day, I'll return the bracelet to Queen Charm with ALL thirteen charms," she told Alfie.

And she closed the lid.

Sesame looked again at the picture painted on it. She now saw that the circle in the picture was a bracelet – EXACTLY like the one she'd found in Karisma. And those thirteen symbols? Sesame was sure it was a code.

"I'm going to crack it or bust!" she said. And went to find a pencil and paper.

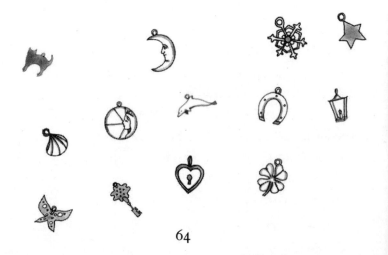

Can you crack the code before Sesame?
Each symbol represents a letter.
CLUE: First, work around the outer circle of symbols to solve the puzzle.

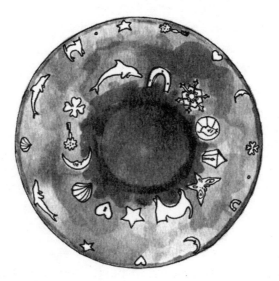

Jewellery box code: A – heart   B – horseshoe   C – star
D – crown   E – dolphin   F – pumpkin   G – fairy   H – key
I – candle   J – coin   K– unicorn   L – shell   M – clover
N – mermaid   O – butterfly   P – gate   Q – sun   R – moon
S – troll   T – cat   U – witch   V – tree   W – snowflake
X – dragon   Y – lantern   Z – flower (poppy)

Later, Sesame was in the kitchen with her gran. Lossy was busy preparing supper and Sesame had fed Chips and Pins. The kittens had just settled down to the serious business of washing and Sesame sat watching them, deep in thought.

"Pass the butter," said Lossy, vigorously mashing a pot of potatoes. When Sesame didn't respond, she looked up. Her granddaughter was miles away!

"Hell-lo. Anyone there?" said Lossy, waving.

Sesame laughed.

"Sorry. What did you say?"

"Everything all right?" said Lossy, reaching for the butter. She knew Sesame's moods so well. Ever since her mother had died, Lossy had helped to bring her up. They were very close.

"Mmm," said Sesame.

"Mmm what?" said Lossy, scooping creamy potatoes into a bowl. There was *something* on Sesame's mind, she was sure.

"G-r-a-n," began Sesame slowly. "Do you believe in . . . do you think there are . . . other worlds?"

"Phew!" said Lossy. "Now there's a question. You been reading those spacey sci-fi books?"

"No," said Sesame. "I mean *real* worlds with real people and . . . things."

Lossy gave this some careful thought. Sesame was so like Poppy, always questioning and wanting to find out more.

"Well, I don't see why not," she said.

And for the time being that was that. There were a million things Sesame wanted to tell Lossy. But she couldn't. Not yet. Not until she'd worked out what had really happened.

It had all begun with that top in the window. She was so *sure* it had been there. And, if it hadn't been for the bracelet, she would have thought she'd imagined it all.

But the bracelet WAS here, in her jewellery box. As real, as real as could be!

After supper Lossy switched on the television to watch the news. Chips and Pins were asleep and Sesame realised she was sleepy too.

"What time will Dad be home?" she said, yawning.

"Late," said Lossy. "He's at that football match, remember?"

Sesame was about to say goodnight, when she caught snippets of a news item on the TV. The newscaster was saying something about . . . *our*

She was keen to know what it was all about, so she waited to see. Apparently, a special organisation had been set up to rescue homeless apes. The rainforest, where they lived, was being cleared for palm oil crops. The apes had nowhere to live and were starving.

"I read about that this morning," said Sesame.

Then some pictures of orphan orangutans appeared on the screen.

"Poor little mites!" said Lossy. "Thank goodness someone's taking care of them."

"Yes," said Sesame. "I wish I could too!"

And suddenly a vision of Hob and Fig flashed through her head. What had happened to Hob? She said she would deal with that gribb . . . Sesame couldn't bear to think about that awful creature and shut her eyes.

"Look at you," said Lossy, "you're half asleep. Now off to bed with you!"

So Sesame kissed her gran and went upstairs.

There was a bag from **TIP TOPS** under her pillow that she hadn't noticed earlier. Sesame read the note attached to it:

Dear Ses,
Forgot to give this to you this morning.
Hope you like it.
Love,
Dad xx

Inside was the bright red top with the sparkly heart. And when Sesame picked it up, a sprinkling of silver dust fell to the floor . . .

Twelve

The Silversmith sighs. The first of the thirteen candles flickers and goes out. Twelve candles remain lit. It's a start. The bracelet has been found with the heart clinging to it. Sesame's quest has begun!

The Silversmith knows Sesame will return to Karisma. When she does, she will learn about the magic of the charms and how important it is to find them all. She has the gift to seek and she must continue her search.

Already there are signs that Karisma is changing, because without the bracelet, the balance of nature is awry. And everyone has been talking about the change in the weather! How, without warning, the gentle summer rains have suddenly turned into torrents; how the crops, ready for harvest, have been ruined by floods.

And only today she's noticed the silver pool – it's lower than she's ever known! What will happen if it dries up? What if there is no more silver? But that's another story! It must keep for another day.

Acknowledgments

I owe a debt of gratitude to all those who have worked behind the scenes at Orion Children's Books and beyond to bring the *Charmseekers* books and their thirteen delightful charms to you. Since it would take more space than this edition allows to mention individuals by name, suffice it to say that I'm hugely grateful to my publishers and everyone involved with the publication of this series. In particular, my special thanks go to: my publisher, Fiona Kennedy, for her faith in believing I could write way beyond my own expectations. Her creative, tactful and skilful editing kept Sesame Brown on the right track and helped me to write a better story; my agent, Rosemary Sandberg; Jenny Glencross and Jane Hughes (Editorial); Alex Nicholas and Helen Speedy (Rights) Loulou Clark and Helen Ewing (Design); Clare Hennessy (Production); Jessica Killingley and Jo Dawson (Marketing); Pandora White (Orion Audio Books); Imogen Adams (Website designer – www.hammerinheels.com); Neil Pymer, the *real* Spinner Shindigs, for kind permission to use his name; and last, but by no means least, a million thanks go to my husband Tom for his inexhaustible patience, critical appraisal and support along the way.

Georgie Adams